U.S. HOLIDAYS

Celebrate Memorial Day

by Melissa Ferguson

PEBBLE
a capstone imprint

First Facts are published by Pebble,
1710 Roe Crest Drive, North Mankato, Minnesota 56003
www.mycapstone.com

Library of Congress Cataloging-in-Publication Data
Library of Congress Cataloging-in-Publication data is available on the Library of Congress website.
978-1-9771-0266-9 (library binding)
978-1-9771-0530-1 (paperback)
978-1-9771-0283-6 (eBook PDF)

Editorial Credits
Mandy Robbins, editor; Cynthia Della-Rovere, designer; Pam Mitsakos, media researcher; Tori Abraham, production specialist

Photo Credits
Alamy: National Geographic Creative, 19; Getty Images: Jeff Greenberg, 20–21, Philip James Corwin, Cover, Sygma/Jeffrey Markowitz, 6–7; Newscom: Xinhua News Agency/Wang Ping, 17; Shutterstock: Allen J.M. Smith, 13, Bokeh Blur Background, Design Element, Duda Vasilii, Design Element, Everett Historical, 8–9, 10–11, Glynnis Jones, 4, sharpner, 1 (bottom), Zoran Karapancev, 3 (bottom left), 15

Printed and bound in the United States of America.
PA49

Table of Contents

What Is Memorial Day?

Americans celebrate Memorial Day the last Monday in May. For many people, this means enjoying a long weekend. But Memorial Day is important for a different reason. It's a time to honor ***veterans*** who have died in battle.

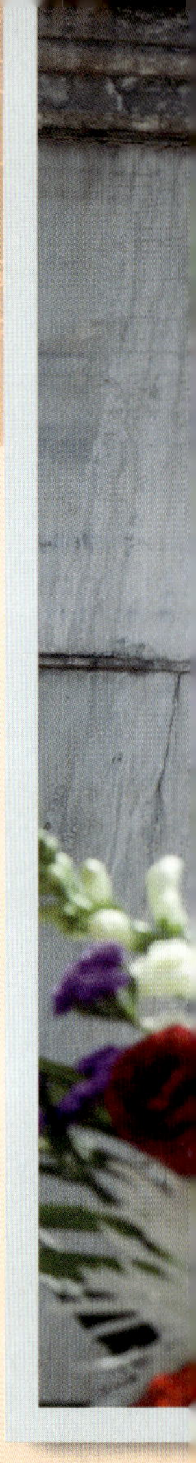

veteran—a person who served in the armed forces

People place flowers on graves to remember loved ones on Memorial Day.

Fact Memorial Day is different from Veterans Day. Veterans Day honors all U.S. veterans, past and present.

Memorial Day is a ***federal*** holiday. It honors military members who have died. People in the military help keep America safe and free. More than 1 million Americans have died in war since 1775.

Less than 10 percent of Americans are veterans.

federal—relating to the U.S. government

60 5673

How Memorial Day Became a Holiday

Memorial Day began after the Civil War (1861-1865). This war was a battle between America's northern and southern states. The states didn't agree on issues, such as states' rights and ***slavery***.

Abraham Lincoln was president during the Civil War. He wanted America to stay a united country.

slavery—the owning of other people; slaves are forced to work without pay

Fact More soldiers died during the Civil War than in any other war in U.S. history.

The Battle of Shiloh was one of many battles fought during the Civil War.

Lincoln gave a speech during the Civil War called the Gettysburg Address. It honored the soldiers who had died.

The North won the war in 1865. America was united again. In 1868 Decoration Day began as a way to remember Civil War soldiers. People put flowers on soldiers' graves.

Lincoln gave the Gettysburg Address where Civil War soldiers were buried.

Over the next 100 years, America fought in many wars. Many men and women in the military died. Americans wanted a way to honor those who died in these wars. Over time, Decoration Day became known as Memorial Day. In 1971 Memorial Day became a federal holiday.

The Uniform Monday Holiday Act

Before 1968 Memorial Day was celebrated on May 30. In 1968 the government passed the Uniform Monday Holiday Act. This law moved some holidays, including Memorial Day, to a Monday. This change gave many American workers a long weekend.

ARTHUR W FIELD
MSGT US AIR FORCE
WORLD WAR II KOREA

Sites and Symbols of Memorial Day

Memorial Day has special ***symbols***. One is the U.S. flag. The American flag is a symbol of freedom. ***Wreaths*** are another symbol of Memorial Day. Wreaths show respect for those who have died. Wreaths and flags are used to decorate the graves of U.S. veterans.

symbol—an object that stands for something else

wreath—a ring of flowers or branches; wreaths are often laid on graves or memorials

Memorial Day also includes the National Moment of Remembrance. This moment of silence is to remember those who died serving our country. The ***tradition*** started in 2000. At 3:00 p.m., ***eastern time***, Americans join together in one minute of silent respect for soldiers who have died.

Arlington National Cemetery

Arlington National Cemetery is near Washington, D.C. More than 400,000 veterans are buried there. Each day, guards at the cemetery honor unknown soldiers who died in wars. On Memorial Day, there are large events to honor all soldiers who have died serving the country.

Special military ceremonies are held all over the country on Memorial Day.

tradition—a custom, idea, or belief passed down through time

eastern time—the time zone along the United States' east coast

How You Can Celebrate Memorial Day

Most people don't go to work or school on Memorial Day. They celebrate the holiday in many ways. People visit cemeteries and place flowers or wreaths on graves. Some communities hold parades or picnics. Others have speeches and concerts.

Fact During World War I (1914–1918), red poppies grew at the site of a bloody battle. Now red poppy flowers are often used to honor fallen soldiers.

MEMORIAL DAY

You can honor those who died in wars too. You can go to a Memorial Day parade. Your family could visit a cemetery together. You could take a moment of silence to show you care on Memorial Day.

National Memorial Day Parade, in Washington D.C.

Tuskegee Airmen who made the ultimate sacrifice for freedom in World War II

Glossary

cemetery (SEM-uh-ter-ee)—a place where dead people are buried

eastern time (EES-turn TYME)—the time zone along the United States' east coast

federal (FED-ur-uhl)—relating to the U.S. government

slavery (SLAY-vur-ee)—the owning of other people; slaves are forced to work without pay

symbol (SIM-buhl)—an object that stands for something else

tradition (truh-DISH-uhn)—a custom, idea, or belief passed down through time

veteran (VET-truhn)—person who served in the armed forces

wreath (REETH)—a ring of flowers or branches; wreaths are often laid on graves or memorials

Read More

Berne, Emma Carlson. *Memorial Day.* North Mankato, Minn.: Cantata Learning, 2018.

Koestler-Grack, Rachel A. *Memorial Day.* Celebrating Holidays. Minneapolis: Bellwether Media, Inc., 2018.

Lake, Kirsten. *Why Do We Celebrate Memorial Day?* Celebrating U.S. Holidays. New York: PowerKids Press, 2018.

Internet Sites

Use FactHound to find Internet sites related to this book.

Visit www.facthound.com

Just type in 9781977102669 and go.

Critical Thinking Questions

1. Why do we celebrate Memorial Day?
2. How is Day different from Veterans Day?
3. What are two ways to honor veterans who died for our country?

Index

U.S. HOLIDAYS

Celebrate Constitution Day

by Yvonne Pearson

PEBBLE
a capstone imprint

First Facts are published by Pebble,
1710 Roe Crest Drive, North Mankato, Minnesota 56003
www.mycapstone.com

Library of Congress Cataloging-in-Publication Data
Library of Congress Cataloging-in-Publication data is available on the Library of Congress website.
ISBN 978-1-9771-0268-3 (library binding)
ISBN 978-1-9771-0531-8 (paperback)
ISBN 978-1-9771-0284-3 (eBook PDF)

Editorial Credits
Mandy Robbins, editor; Cynthia Della-Rovere, designer; Pam Mitsakos, media researcher; Tori Abraham, production specialist

Photo Credits
Alamy: Michael Ventura, Cover; Newscom: akg-images, 13, Polaris/Scott Houston, 3 (bottom left), 21; Shutterstock: BigAlBaloo, 17, Bokeh Blur Background, Design Element, Charles Haire, 11, Chris Parypa Photography, 6–7, Duda Vasilii, Design Element, Ekaterina_Minaeva, 14–15, eurobanks, 4–5, Everett Historical, 8–9, jiawangkun, 18–19, sharpner, 1 (bottom)

Printed and bound in the United States of America.
PA49

Table of Contents

Celebrating Democracy

Americans celebrate Independence Day on July 4th. But they have a different holiday in September. On September 17th, they celebrate the signing of the U.S. Constitution. This document made the United States government a *democracy*.

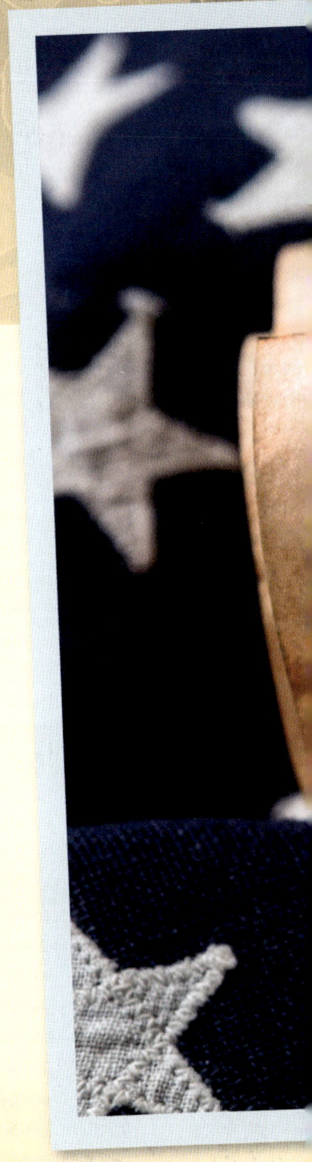

democracy—a kind of government in which the people make decisions by voting

a copy of the United States Constitution

Fact Constitution Day is also called Citizenship Day.

The Constitution explains how the U.S. government works. It also gives basic rights to all ***citizens***.

Constitution Day is a day to celebrate the nation's government. It is also a time to honor the 39 men who signed the U.S. Constitution.

Fact The U.S. Constitution is less than 5,000 words long.

citizen—a member of a country or state who has the right to live there

The History of the Constitution

During the *Revolutionary* War (1775–1783), the states formed a government. It gave the states much of the power. But it made the nation's government too weak.

State *representatives* met in 1787 to form a new government. After nine months of *debates*, they created the U.S. Constitution.

revolution—an attempt to overthrow a government and replace it with a new system

representative—someone who is chosen to act or speak for others

debate—a discussion between two sides with different ways of thinking on a subject

George Washington speaks at the Convention of 1787 to create a new government.

Some Americans thought the new Constitution did not protect people's ***rights***. Leaders then passed the Bill of Rights. These ***amendments*** guard citizens' rights and freedoms. The First Amendment protects many rights. They include free speech and freedom of religion.

Fact Americans have added 27 amendments to the Constitution.

rights—something that the law says you can have or do, as in the right to vote

amendment—a change made to a law or a legal document

Freedoms for All Americans

When the U.S. Constitution was written, only white men who owned land could vote. African-Americans held as slaves and all women could not. Amendments changed that. In 1865 the Thirteenth Amendment freed enslaved people. In 1870 the Fifteenth Amendment gave African-American men the right to vote. Women won the right to vote in 1920 with the Nineteenth Amendment.

Changes to the Holiday

Constitution Day started in 1940 as "I Am an American Day." It was a day to celebrate being a U.S. citizen. It was the third Sunday in May. The idea for the holiday came from William Randolph Hearst's 1939 film. It was called *I Am an American*.

William Randolph Hearst

In the 1950s, Olga T. Weber wanted the holiday changed to September 17th. The Constitution was signed that day. She spoke to local leaders in Louisville, Ohio. They agreed to change the date in 1952. By 1953 she had convinced U.S. Congress to change it too. The holiday became Citizenship Day.

17
18
Citizenship
Day
24
25

Louise Leigh thought the Constitution deserved a holiday too. She was proud of the freedoms it gave Americans. Leigh started a group called Constitution Day, Inc. It pushed lawmakers to make a holiday for the Constitution. In 2004 September 17th became Constitution Day and Citizenship Day.

CONSTITUTION DAY
E PLURIBUS UNUM
September 17th

How Americans Celebrate

The Constitution was signed in Philadelphia, Pennsylvania. The National Constitution Center is there. It holds a big celebration with birthday cake and debates.

Public schools teach about the Constitution on Constitution Day. Students learn the rights and responsibilities it gives all citizens.

The National Constitution Center in Philadelphia, Pennsylvania

Americans also celebrate new citizens on September 17. People born in the United States are U.S. citizens. ***Immigrants*** can also become citizens. There are 10 steps in this process. They include an interview and a test. Then new citizens go through a ceremony. Many are held on Constitution Day.

Fact If a child's parent becomes a U.S. citizen, the child can also be a citizen.

immigrant—a person who leaves one country and settles in another

Guarding the Constitution

The U.S. Constitution is held at the National *Archives* in Washington, D.C. Each day, hundreds of people come to see it. The Constitution is more than 200 years old. It is kept under bulletproof glass to keep it from getting damaged. At night it is kept in an underground safe made of steel and concrete.

archive—a place where historical papers are stored

Glossary

amendment (uh-MEND-muhnt)—a change made to a law or a legal document

archive (AR-kyv)—a place where historical papers are stored

citizen (SI-tuh-zuhn)—a member of a country or state who has the right to live there

debate (di-BATE)—a discussion between two sides with different ways of thinking on a subject

democracy (di-MAH-kruh-see)—a government in which the people make decisions by voting

immigrant (IM-uh-gruhnt)—a person who leaves one country and settles in another

representative (rep-ri-ZEN-tuh-tiv)—someone who is chosen to act or speak for others

revolution (rev-uh-LOO-shun)—an attempt to overthrow a government and replace it with a new system

right (RITE)—something that the law says you can have or do, as in the right to vote

Read More

Clay, Kathryn. *The U.S. Constitution: Introducing Primary Sources.* Smithsonian Little Explorer. North Mankato, Minn.: Capstone Press, 2016.

Demuth, Patricia. *What Is the Constitution?* What Was? New York: Penguin Workshop, an imprint of Penguin Random House, 2018.

DeRubertis, Barbara. *Let's Celebrate Constitution Day.* Holidays & Heroes. New York: The Kane Press, 2015.

Internet Sites

Use FactHound to find Internet sites related to this book.

Visit www.facthound.com

Just type in 9781977102683 and go.

Critical Thinking Questions

1. Why is the U.S. Constitution important?
2. Why did people want to add amendments to the Constitution?
3. How can you celebrate Constitution Day?

Index